Merry Fish-mas

Swim into more

PuRRmaiDs

adventures!

PuRRmaids

8

Merry Fish-mas

by Sudipta Bardhan-Quallen

illustrations by Vivien Wu

A STEPPING STONE BOOK™
Random House 🏠 New York

Text copyright © 2020 by Sudipta Bardhan-Quallen
Cover art copyright © 2020 by Andrew Farley
Interior illustrations copyright © 2020 by Vivien Wu

Visit us on the Web!
rhcbooks.com

Educators and librarians, for a variety of teaching tools, visit us at
RHTeachersLibrarians.com

Library of Congress Cataloging-in-Publication Data
Names: Bardhan-Quallen, Sudipta, author. I Wu, Vivien, illustrator.
Title: Merry Fish-mas / by Sudipta Bardhan-Quallen;
illustrations by Vivien Wu.
Description: New York: Random House Children's Books, [2020] I
Series: Purrmaids; volume 8 I "A Stepping Stone Book." I Audience: Ages 6–9. I
Summary: "All of Kittentail Cove is excited for Fish-mas, but things begin
to go wrong when Coral is unable to mail her little brother's letter
to Santa Paws in time"—Provided by publisher.
Identifiers: LCCN 2019027909 I ISBN 978-1-9848-9610-0 (trade pbk.) I
ISBN 978-1-9848-9611-7 (lib. bdg.) I ISBN 978-1-9848-9612-4 (ebook)
Subjects: CYAC: Mermaids—Fiction. I Cats—Fiction. I
Brothers and sisters—Fiction. I Christmas—Fiction.
Classification: LCC PZ7.B25007 Mg 2020 I DDC [Fic]—dc23

Printed in the United States of America
10 9 8 7 6 5 4 3
First Edition

This book has been officially leveled by using
the F&P Text Level Gradient™ Leveling System.

Random House Children's Books supports the
First Amendment and celebrates the right to read.

To Audrey,
a girl of many questions

1

It was a cold December morning. Coral was out of her oyster-shell bed even earlier than usual. Today was Room Eel-Twelve's Fish-mas party, and she was too excited to sleep.

Coral got up and brushed her orange fur. She put on her green Fish-mas sweater that said HAPPY PAW-LIDAYS. Then she snapped on her friendship bracelet. It was very special because her best friends in the ocean, Angel and Shelly, wore matching ones. The charms reminded them of all the fun adventures they'd had together.

"Fish-mas is my favorite time of year!" Coral purred at breakfast.

Purrmaids celebrated lots of holidays, like Founder's Day, Ground Hogfish Day, and International Talk Like a Pirate Day. Each holiday had its own traditions, and there was at least one paw-some thing about each one. But for Coral, Fish-mas was the most fin-credible. She loved Fish-mas more than all the other holidays put together.

"It's my favorite, too," replied her

brother, Shrimp. "Fish-mas presents are the best!"

Papa laughed. But Mama shook her head. "Fish-mas is about more than just presents, Shrimp," she said. "It's about spending time with your family and your friends. It's about being grateful for the good things in your life. It's about spreading joy and happiness to everyone you know."

Shrimp lowered his eyes. "I know, Mama," he mumbled.

Coral leaned toward her brother and elbowed him. "Mama is right," she whispered, "but the presents are great."

Shrimp grinned.

Mama carried a plate of seaweed pancakes to the table. She pointed to the piece of paper in front of Shrimp. "Is that your letter to Santa Paws?" she asked. "We have to put it in the snail mail today or he won't get it in time."

"I already sent mine," Coral said. "I didn't want it to be late." Being late was against the rules, and she hated breaking the rules!

"I'm almost done," Shrimp said. "I just need a few more minutes."

Mama checked the clock on the wall. "I have some Fish-mas errands to do," she explained, "so I have to leave now."

Shrimp frowned. "Can I have ten more minutes?" When Mama shook her head, he asked, "Can you take it, Papa?"

Papa said, "Sorry, but I have to go get our Fish-mas sea fan today. If I don't, we won't have anything to decorate tomorrow on Fish-mas Eve."

Every year, purrmaids all around

Kittentail Cove decorated their town to spread Fish-mas spirit. They hung garlands made of kelp, pearls, and sea glass. They carved ice sculptures of Santa Paws and Jack Furr-ost. They made ornaments out of shells and starfish to decorate Fish-mas sea fans in their homes.

Most of the Fish-mas sea fans in Kittentail Cove were about as tall as a grown-up purrmaid. But there were always two giant sea fans in town. One was in front of the Kittentail Cove Library. The other was at Coral's house.

"Are you going to get the biggest Fish-mas sea fan you can find?" Shrimp asked.

Papa grinned. "I always do, don't I?"

Shrimp looked down at his letter. "How will I get this to Santa Paws?" he whined.

"Don't worry, Shrimp," Mama said. "Santa Paws has been keeping an eye on you all year long. He already knows what you'd write in your letter."

"But I changed my mind at the last minute," Shrimp said. "He can't know that."

"Yes, he can," Mama replied. "It's part of the magic of Fish-mas."

Shrimp didn't look like he agreed with Mama. Suddenly, Coral had an idea. "I can mail it," she said. "We swim past the post office on our way to sea school." She turned to her parents. "You two go ahead. I'll drop off Shrimp's letter."

"You will?" Shrimp asked. "Thank you! You're my favorite sister!"

"I'm your only sister," Coral purred, smiling.

"Thank you for taking this responsibility, Coral," Mama said.

"It's a truly Fish-mas-y thing to do," Papa added.

"I hope Santa Paws is watching now," Coral joked, "so he brings me something extra special!"

"I couldn't send a letter to Santa Paws without you," Shrimp said, "so you deserve it."

Coral felt her face getting warmer. "I'm happy to do it, buddy," she said. She ruffled Shrimp's fur. "Think of this as my Fish-mas gift to you."

Shrimp scowled. "Wait! You are going to get me *another* present, too, right? A real present?"

Coral laughed. "You'll have to wait until Fish-mas morning to see!" she said.

2

While Shrimp worked on his letter, Coral finished her breakfast. Then she glanced at her brother. He was still writing. *I hope he hurries,* she thought.

"Did you pack your gift for today, Coral?" Papa asked.

"I'll double-check now," Coral said. She reached into her backpack and held up a small package. "Here it is! I wrapped it in red and green seaweed so it would look especially meow-y!"

"Is it for me?" Shrimp asked.

Coral shook her head. "Not this one, buddy," she said. "This is for my class's white elephant seal gift exchange."

"What's that?" Shrimp asked.

"Everyone brings in a present," Coral explained. "Then we put all the presents in a big pile and everyone chooses one. You don't know who brought it in or what it is, so it's a surprise."

"I think a white elephant seal gift exchange is such a nice idea," Papa purred.

"Ms. Harbor always has great ideas!" Coral replied.

"What are you bringing?" Shrimp asked.

Coral opened one corner of the package so Shrimp could peek in. "It's a Fish-mas decoration," Coral said. "I painted a cone shell red. I used snail slime to stick small pearls around the bottom and one on the tip."

"It looks like the hat that Santa Paws wears!" Shrimp squealed.

"Exactly!" Coral said. "I know that the white elephant seal gifts can end up with anyone. But it would be nice if Shelly or Angel picked this one." She put the present back into her bag and floated over to her brother. "Are you done with your letter?"

"Just one more minute," Shrimp said.

Coral checked the clock. "I'm going to be late! Hurry up!"

"I'm hurrying!" Shrimp exclaimed.

Coral played with her bracelet as she waited for her brother. She sometimes did

that when she was worried, and right now she was worried about the time.

Finally, Shrimp put his sea pen down. He folded the letter and put it in an envelope.

"I'll take that," Coral said. She almost snatched it from his paws. "I have to go!"

"Thank you for mailing it!" Shrimp shouted.

Coral was already rushing out the door. *Maybe if I swim fast enough,* she thought, *going to the post office won't be a purr-oblem!*

Angel and Shelly were waiting for Coral in Leondra's Square. They were both dressed up in Fish-mas sweaters for the class party. Shelly was wearing a silver sweater decorated with red starfish. Angel's red sweater said MEOW-Y AND BRIGHT in big gold letters.

Coral barely stopped swimming when she reached her friends.

"We've been here fur-ever!" Angel said.

"I know!" Coral replied. "I'm sorry. I had to wait for my brother to finish his letter to Santa Paws. And now I'm supposed to bring it to the post office!"

"Don't worry, Coral," Shelly purred.

"We have enough time. We can drop it off *and* get to school before the bell."

That was what Coral thought, too. Until the post office came into view.

On most days, there were maybe three or four purrmaids waiting to mail something. But today, the line stretched out into the street.

Coral frowned. "We can't wait in that line," she said. "It would take too long!"

"We could be a little late for sea school," Angel suggested. "We'll just explain what happened. I think Ms. Harbor will understand."

Coral shook her head. "Being late is against the rules."

"Why don't we plan to come back after school?" Shelly said. "We have to swim back this way. This afternoon, we'd have plenty of time to wait our turn."

Coral bit her lip. She purr-omised Shrimp she'd mail his letter. But she didn't purr-omise to do it in the morning. "That's a good plan, Shelly," she said.

"Then what are we waiting for?" Angel asked. "Last one there's a rotten skeg!"

3

Soon the girls arrived at sea school. They hurried toward Room Eel-Twelve. They found Ms. Harbor decorating the classroom Fish-mas sea fan.

"Meow-y Fish-mas, Ms. Harbor," Coral said as they swam into the room.

"Meow-y Fish-mas!" Ms. Harbor replied. When she spun around, Coral giggled at Ms. Harbor's Fish-mas sweater. It had a picture of a toad in a Santa Paws hat with the words MEET ME UNDER THE MISTLE-TOAD.

"You're not laughing at my sweater, are you?" Ms. Harbor asked, scowling. But then she winked and Coral knew she was just kidding.

"It is paw-sitively ugly," Coral said, "but I think that's what you wanted!"

"Well, the only thing better than a purr-ty Fish-mas sweater is a paw-sitively ugly one!" Ms. Harbor joked.

All the purrmaids laughed. Then Ms. Harbor purred, "I'm glad you're here. I want to finish decorating before our Fish-mas party."

"We'll help you," Angel said.

"Should we put our white elephant seal presents under the sea fan first?" Shelly asked.

"No," Ms. Harbor said. She pointed to

a large red bag on her desk. "Put them in there. I want to make sure no one knows what your gifts look like."

"We shouldn't see each other's presents, then," Coral said. "Let's take turns. I'll go first."

Angel and Shelly turned away from Ms. Harbor's desk and started hanging ornaments on the Fish-mas sea fan. When she was sure they weren't looking, Coral carefully took her present out of her backpack. She placed it inside the bag.

"Your turn, Angel," Coral said. She floated next to Shelly and started to decorate.

A moment later, Angel said, "Shelly, you can go ahead."

Slowly, all the students of Room Eel-Twelve swam through the classroom door. By the time the bell rang, everyone's presents were put away, and the Fish-mas sea fan was completely decorated.

"Just one more thing," Ms. Harbor said. She reached up and placed a golden starfish on the very top of the Fish-mas sea fan. "Purr-fect!"

"Can we start the Fish-mas party now?" Baker asked.

"Especially the part with the gifts?" Taylor added.

Everyone giggled.

"I think that's a fin-tastic idea," Ms. Harbor said. She gently emptied the red bag under the Fish-mas sea fan. The presents were all different colors, shapes, and sizes. "Now, each of you needs to pick a number so we know whose turn it is to pick a gift." She took a green bag out of her desk drawer. "No peeking!"

Ms. Harbor went around the room, holding the green bag open for her students. One by one, they reached into the bag and pulled out a small shell. Each shell had a number on it.

Angel looked at her shell and grinned. "I picked number one!" she exclaimed.

"And I picked number three!" Shelly said. She held her shell up to show everyone.

It was Coral's turn to choose a shell. She grabbed one from the very bottom of the bag. When she looked at the number, she frowned.

"What did you get, Coral?" Shelly asked.

Coral turned the shell so her friends could see. "I'm number fifteen." There were only fifteen students in the class, so Coral would be the last one to select a white elephant seal gift. Since there would only be one present left, it wasn't even a choice.

I'm having the worst luck

today, Coral thought. But then she reminded herself, *Fish-mas isn't just about getting stuff.* She wouldn't have any choices by the time they got to her turn, but Shelly and Angel would. *That means my best friends have a good chance of picking the one I made!* Coral smiled at the thought.

The purrmaids of Room Eel-Twelve lined up in order in front of the Fish-mas sea fan. Angel was going to go first, so she was at the front of the line. Coral was all the way at the end.

"Remember," Ms. Harbor purred, "don't grab the gift that you brought in." She nodded toward Angel. "Get us started."

Angel barely looked at all the packages before she swam straight to the largest one. "I want this one!" she said. She swam back to her desk with her present. "Hurry up, everyone! I really want to open this!"

Coral bit her lip. Angel didn't choose her present.

Adrianna took the next turn. She pawed through the pile, pushing some packages away. *I guess those are the ones she knows she* doesn't *want*, Coral thought.

Luckily, Adrianna pushed Coral's present away, too! That meant Shelly still had a chance to pick it.

Adrianna finally selected a package that was wrapped in silver and gold seaweed dotted with tiny pearls. "This one looks fancy!" she said.

Shelly swam up to the pile next. She reached toward Coral's gift. Coral thought, *I hope Shelly picks mine!*

But at the last moment, Shelly changed her mind. She grabbed the package next to Coral's and swam to her desk.

Coral gulped. *So far,* she thought, *this has not been a very Meow-y Fish-mas!*

4

The rest of the purrmaids kept choosing gifts and returning to their desks. Coral pretended to look out the window at the Fish-mas decorations in the schoolyard. But she was really trying to hide her face. She didn't want anyone to see that she was upset.

"Coral," Ms. Harbor said happily, "you're next."

Coral backed away from the window. "Sorry," she mumbled. She turned to the Fish-mas sea fan. And her eyes grew wide. "Why are there two presents left?" she asked. "Did someone miss their turn?"

"No," Ms. Harbor replied. "There are sixteen purrmaids in the class, and you are number fifteen."

"Sixteen?" Coral said. "There are only fifteen students here."

Ms. Harbor winked. "I'm part of the class, too! I'm number sixteen!"

"Go ahead, Coral," Shelly purred.

Coral nodded and swam to the gifts. One of the packages was wrapped in red and green seaweed. *I can't take that one,* Coral thought. *It's mine!* So she reached for the other package and grinned. Since Ms. Harbor was the only one left, she would get Coral's present. That was just as nice as one of her best friends picking it!

As soon as Coral sat down at her desk, Ms. Harbor said, "It's time!"

The students began to open their white elephant seal gifts. Angel quickly ripped the seaweed wrapping paper to shreds. She made a huge mess, but that never bothered her. "Look at this!" she shouted. She held up a red-and-green scarf. "This is purr-fect for a chilly Fish-mas season."

Shelly carefully removed the wrapping on her package. She made sure nothing got torn. That was because Shelly disliked messes as much as Angel liked them! "Wow!" Shelly exclaimed. "Coconut snowball cookies! These are my favorite."

"Your turn, Coral," Angel said.

Coral pulled the ribbon on her present to undo the bow. She opened the lid of the box and lifted something out. It was a hat with a mistle-toad on it. It matched her teacher's Fish-mas sweater.

Ms. Harbor swam up behind Coral. "Do you like it?" she asked. "I made it myself."

Coral beamed. "I love it!" She pointed to the unopened package in Ms. Harbor's paws. "Now you have to open yours and tell me if you like it."

Ms. Harbor's jaw dropped. "Did I pick your gift?" she asked.

"And I picked yours!" Coral replied.

Ms. Harbor said, "I feel very lucky already." She quickly unwrapped the gift. "This is a beautiful Fish-mas ornament, Coral!" she purred. "Did you make it?"

Coral nodded.

"I'm going to hang it on our Fish-mas sea fan!" Ms. Harbor announced. "It will be a part of this classroom every Fish-mas from now on."

Coral smiled so hard her cheeks hurt. She put her mistle-toad hat on and said, "Meow-y Fish-mas, everyone!"

Ms. Harbor brought out a tray of Fish-mas treats. There were cups of green and red seaweed salad, star-shaped cookies, and sea urchin sushi rolls topped with water snowflakes. "Is anyone hungry?" she asked.

"It's not a party without food!" Shelly joked.

The students gathered around the Fishmas sea fan with their snacks. As they ate, Ms. Harbor asked, "Did everyone get a chance to write to Santa Paws?"

The purrmaids nodded. Coral quickly swallowed her bite of cookie and said, "My letter is already in the snail mail. I have to drop my brother's letter off this afternoon."

"There was one year, when I was a kitten," Ms. Harbor said, "I forgot to mail my letter in time. I remember trying to stay up until midnight to hand it to him."

"Wasn't that past your bedtime?" Coral wondered.

"Yes, it was!" Ms. Harbor replied. "Way past my bedtime."

"Did you stay awake until he got there?" Angel asked.

Ms. Harbor chuckled and shook her head. "No, I fell asleep in front of the Fish-mas sea fan."

"So you didn't get anything from Santa Paws that year?" Shelly asked.

"Actually, I did," Ms. Harbor purred. "In fact, he brought me a book about taking care of pet crabs. I didn't even know I wanted that! But a few weeks later, my parents got me a pet crab. I knew what to do because of that book. Santa Paws knew exactly what I needed—even though I didn't!"

"So even if we don't write to Santa Paws, he knows what to do for Fish-mas?" Cascade asked.

"In my opinion," Ms. Harbor answered, "Santa Paws knows more than any of us thinks he does." She winked. "But it's still a good idea to get your letters in the mail!"

That's what I'll do for Shrimp, Coral thought. She wanted her brother to have a wonderful Fish-mas. *I don't want to take any chances with his letter!*

5

Before Coral knew it, the bell was ringing. The school day was over.

"Enjoy Fish-mas break," Ms. Harbor purred. "Happy Paw-lidays!"

Coral grabbed Shrimp's letter and swung her backpack over her shoulder. "Let's go to the post office," she said to her friends.

"Hopefully, the line won't be as long now," Shelly said.

The girls swam down Canal Street. Along the way, they passed Meow Meadow. There was a group of Fish-mas carolers in front of the gazebo. They were singing "Have Yourself a Meow-y Little Fish-mas."

"I forgot about Fish-mas caroling," Angel said. "We haven't done that yet."

Coral scowled. "Maybe after we mail the letter." She started to leave. But Shelly stayed behind. "Are you coming?" Coral asked.

"Please, can we join the carolers?" Shelly begged.

Coral bit her lip. Everyone knew that Shelly loved to sing. She finally said, "Okay. Just a few songs, though. We have to get to the post office before it closes."

Shelly gave Coral a hug. "Thank you!" she exclaimed. She took Coral's paw and led her toward the carolers.

The girls sang along to "Jingle Shell Rock," "Happy Paw-lidays," and "Santa Paws Is Coming to Town." By then, Coral was having so much fun she didn't want to stop.

"We can come back after we mail the letter," Shelly said.

"You're right," Coral said.

"Can we quickly stop at the library?" Angel asked. "The Fish-mas sea fan ceremony is going to start soon. My mom is

going to put the topper on the Fish-mas
sea fan this year."

"I don't know if we have time," Coral
said.

"We stopped to carol for Shelly!"
Angel whined. "Please? It'll only take a
few minutes."

Coral sighed. Angel loved watching the town Fish-mas sea fan ceremony as much as Shelly loved caroling. Coral loved her best friends and wanted them to be happy. This year was even more special to Angel because her mother would be putting the final touch on the Fish-mas sea fan. *Fish-mas is when we're supposed to do nice things for the purrmaids we love,* she thought.

"I can't say no to you at Fish-mas," she said.

"Thank you, Coral!" Angel said. "We'll race to the post office right after, I purr-omise."

The three kittens left Meow Meadow. There were already many purrmaids waiting in front of the library. The girls swam through the crowd to get as close to the front as they could.

Mrs. Shore spied them and waved to them to join her. "I'm glad you three are here," she whispered.

"We can only stop for a minute," Angel replied. "We have a job to do for Shrimp."

Luckily, the ceremony was about to start. "It's almost Fish-mas in Kittentail Cove," Mayor Rivers announced. "I'm happy to see so many purrmaids here to celebrate with us. Let's not waste any more time talking. Councilmaid Shore, would you please place the topper on our magnificent Fish-mas sea fan?"

All the purrmaids clapped. Mrs. Shore reached into a box near her tail. She took out an unusual topper.

Most purrmaids placed a starfish on top of their Fish-mas sea fans. Some, like Coral's parents, got a special starfish that could glow in the dark. But Mrs. Shore didn't have a starfish in her paws. She was holding a deep red crown jellyfish. She swam up and gently placed it on the very top of the Fish-mas sea fan. She arranged the tentacles so they fell all around the Fish-mas sea fan. Then she gave the jellyfish a little shake. In a fin-stant, bright blue lights flashed from the jellyfish's body and tentacles.

"Wow!" Coral purred.

"Meow-y Fish-mas, everyone!" Mrs. Shore shouted. The crowd cheered some more.

"That was worth a few minutes, wasn't it?" Angel asked.

Coral nodded. "We don't get to see a light show like that every day."

"You found a purr-fect topper, Mrs. Shore," Shelly said.

Mrs. Shore smiled. "Thank you!" she

replied. "Now can I help you with the job you need to do?"

Coral shook her head. "No, we're all right. We just have to stop at the post office to mail my brother's letter to Santa Paws."

Mrs. Shore's smile disappeared. "I didn't know you had to go to the post office," she said. "That might be a purr-oblem."

"Why?" Angel asked. "It's not far from here."

"No, it's not," Mrs. Shore said. "But it did close early today."

Coral's eyes grew wide. "I didn't know that!" she moaned. "What am I going to do now?"

6

Coral slumped on the steps of the library. She stared at her brother's letter. Angel and Shelly sat on either side of her.

"This is all my fault," Shelly said. "I shouldn't have asked to stop for the Fishmas caroling."

"No, it's my fault," Angel said. "We should have gone straight to the post office after caroling. Then it still might have been open."

Coral shook her head. "This isn't anyone's fault but mine. I shouldn't have stopped anywhere after school. I made a purr-omise to Shrimp. It was my responsibility to make sure I could keep my word."

"What do we do?" Shelly asked.

Coral shrugged.

In the distance, the bells in the Kitten-tail Cove clock tower started to ring. It was five o'clock.

"We all need to get home," Angel said.

Coral nodded.

"But we'll see you at your house tomorrow, right?" Shelly asked.

"It's one of my favorite Fish-mas Eve traditions," Angel added.

Fish-mas Eve was a busy night at Lake

Restaurant. Shelly's parents worked until very late. As a member of the Kittentail Cove Council, Angel's mother had to attend official ceremonies on Fish-mas Eve. That was why Coral, Shelly, and Angel always spent Fish-mas Eve at the Marshes' house.

"Of course," Coral said. "You'll both help us decorate our Fish-mas sea fan."

"Will it be bigger than last year's?" Angel asked, grinning.

"Is the ocean wet?" Coral replied, trying to make a joke. But it didn't work. She still felt sad.

"It sounds like we're going to have a lot of work to do tonight before Santa Paws comes," Shelly said.

"That's it!" Coral exclaimed.

"What?" Angel asked.

"Santa Paws is coming tomorrow!" Coral answered.

Angel and Shelly looked at each other. Then Shelly said, "Everyone knows that."

"Don't you see? This fixes everything!" Coral said. "We don't have to put Shrimp's letter in the snail mail. We can *give* it to Santa Paws tomorrow!"

"You're right!" Angel purred.

"All we have to do is stay up until he arrives, just like Ms. Harbor tried to do," Coral said. "It's past my usual bedtime, but I think it'll be all right just this once."

Shelly giggled. "It must be important if you're willing to break a rule!"

Coral smiled. "I purr-omised Shrimp I'd give Santa Paws his letter. I want to make sure I do."

Angel took one of Coral's paws. Shelly

took the other. "And you'll have us to help you," Angel said. "After all, what are friends for?"

Coral worried about seeing Shrimp when she got home. *What if he asks me about the letter?* She didn't want to lie to him. It would be better if she didn't have to say anything until after she gave the letter to Santa Paws on Fish-mas Eve.

Luckily, Shrimp had so much to tell

his family about his day that he didn't ask any questions. "Our class party was paw-some!" he said. He talked about the decorations, snacks, and music. But he was exhausted from all the excitement. He actually fell asleep at the dinner table!

"We should all get some rest," Mama whispered as she carried Shrimp to his room. "There will be a lot to do tomorrow."

Coral nodded. *I'll need lots of rest for tomorrow night,* she thought. She blew her parents kisses and purred, "Good night!"

🐾 🐾 🐾

For most of Fish-mas Eve, Coral didn't even have a chance to worry about Shrimp's letter. There was so much to do! "I want everything to be purr-fect for Santa Paws!" she kept saying.

The Marsh family pinned their Fish-mas cards to the walls. They hung jingle shells and kelp garlands. And then they started hanging ornaments on the Fish-mas sea fan.

This year, Papa had found the biggest Fish-mas sea fan that Coral had ever seen. It reached the ceiling of the living room! It still wasn't completely decorated when the doorbell rang.

DING-DONG!

Coral rushed to open it. "I've got it, Mama!" she shouted.

Shelly and her mother, Mrs. Lake, were waiting outside. "Come in," Coral said.

"Thank you, Coral," Mrs. Lake said.

Shelly hugged Coral. "Meow-y Fish-mas Eve!" she said.

Coral was about to close the front door when she saw a flash of black-and-white fur. She peeked outside. "Angel, you're here!" she exclaimed.

"Late, of course," Shelly joked.

"Just a little bit late," Angel replied.

"That's only because I rushed her," Mrs. Shore said. She winked at Coral.

Coral led the purrmaids into the living room. As soon as they saw the Fish-mas sea fan, everyone clapped.

"This is the most Fish-mas-y sea fan yet!" Mrs. Shore gasped.

"It's simply fin-credible!" Mrs. Lake added.

Papa smiled. "Thank you. It wasn't easy to find one this size."

"Thank you for hosting the girls on Fish-mas Eve again," Mrs. Shore said.

"It's our pleasure," Mama purred. "Fish-mas is meow-iest when you spend it with good friends."

Coral pulled Shelly and Angel to the side of the room. "Are you still going to help me get Shrimp's letter to Santa Paws?"

"Of course!" Angel agreed.

"It's going to be the best part of Fishmas Eve!" Shelly said.

7

"Are you girls hatching a plan over there?" Papa asked.

The grown-ups chuckled.

"We are!" Coral replied. "Angel and Shelly are going to help me with a special Fish-mas idea."

"You'd better get to work, then," Mrs. Shore said. "You still have to finish decorating the Fish-mas sea fan."

"Your moms will be back before you know it," Mama said.

Coral frowned. "What time will you be here?"

"I'll pick Shelly up after we close the restaurant," Mrs. Lake said. "Maybe around ten o'clock."

"I shouldn't be much later than that," said Mrs. Shore. "I'll be here as soon as all the Cove Council activities are over."

"That's too early!" Coral yelled. She spun to face her friends. "Santa Paws doesn't visit until after midnight."

Shelly and Angel swam toward their mothers.

"We want to wait for Santa Paws," Shelly said.

"Can we stay until he gets here?" Angel asked.

"That might be very late," Mrs. Lake said, frowning.

"Please?" Coral asked. She clasped her paws. "It's really important for me to meet Santa Paws this year. I need help from Shelly and Angel to stay awake until he gets here."

"It's all right with us," Papa purred.

"It might take that long to finish our Fish-mas sea fan," Mama joked.

"I guess our kittens aren't so little any-more," Mrs. Shore said. "I suppose you're old enough to wait up for Santa Paws."

"I agree," Mrs. Lake said. "Just don't fall asleep."

"We won't," Shelly replied.

Angel nodded.

Coral grinned. "That's purr-fect!" she exclaimed. "Thank you!"

The girls waved goodbye to Mrs. Lake and Mrs. Shore. Coral swam to a box of Fish-mas ornaments. "Help me deco-rate," she said. She handed her friends two ornaments each.

As they worked, Shelly asked, "What do you think it will be like to meet Santa Paws?"

"It's going to be paw-sitively paw-some!" Coral answered.

"It will be a lot like meeting Kelpy Sharkson," Angel said. "Maybe even better than that."

Shelly's smile disappeared. She got very serious. "Nothing could be better than meeting Kelpy Sharkson," she said.

Coral giggled. Shelly was Kelpy Sharkson's biggest fan.

The kittens worked on the decorations until it was time for Fish-mas Eve dinner. When Mama called them to eat, the Fish-mas sea fan still had some empty branches! "I need a break," Shelly said.

"I need food!" Angel exclaimed. "This is hard work!"

The girls sat down at the table just as Mama brought out the Fish-mas goosefish. "We also have mashed sea potatoes, sea beet salad, and oysters on the half shell."

"Everything looks yummy, Mrs. Marsh," Shelly said.

Papa carved the goosefish and put a slice on everyone's plate. Shrimp scooped mashed sea potatoes and salad onto plates. Coral gave out oysters.

"Meow-y Fish-mas, everyone," Shrimp said.

Coral wanted to get back to work. She ate very quickly. "Are you done yet?" she asked her friends. "Santa Paws won't visit until all the decorating is finished."

"I want seconds," Angel said. She got herself another slice of goosefish. She didn't notice Coral scowling.

"Don't worry, Coral," Shelly purred. She patted her friend's paw. "We'll get everything done."

"We're all going to help with the Fish-
mas sea fan," Papa said. "Right after
dinner."

Coral sighed. She had to wait for
everyone else. She didn't have a choice.

Mama tapped Coral's shoulder. "Since
you've eaten all you're going to eat, can
you help me with some of the cleanup?"

Coral nodded. She grabbed a stack
of empty bowls from the table. Mama
picked up some plates. They carried them

to the kitchen. As soon as Coral put her bowls down, Mama asked, "What's going on with you? Why do you want to meet Santa Paws so badly?"

Coral bit her lip. "Wh-what do you mean?" she stammered.

Mama put her paws on her hips. She looked right into Coral's eyes. "You're my daughter," she said, "and I know when there's something fishy going on."

Coral felt tears welling in her eyes. She knew she couldn't hide anything from Mama. "It's Shrimp's letter," she said.

"The one you took to the post office?" Mama asked.

Coral nodded. "I tried to mail it. But the post office closed early! I didn't know." She shrugged. "I feel paw-ful. But I know how I can make it better! I can give Santa Paws the letter tonight."

Mama smiled. "That's why you're trying to make everything purr-fect," she said. "And why you, Angel, and Shelly are planning to stay up until midnight."

"Please don't tell Shrimp about my mistake," Coral begged. "I can fix it. He doesn't need to know!"

Mama pulled Coral into a hug. "I think he would enjoy knowing he has a sister who loves him this much," she purred.

"Real Fish-mas magic doesn't have to come from Santa Paws. It can also come from loving each other."

"I know, Mama," Coral said. But Fish-mas magic from your sister wasn't the same as Fish-mas magic from Santa Paws. Grown-ups never understood that!

8

Finally, the rest of the purrmaids finished their Fish-mas Eve dinner. Coral led them back to the living room. Together, they decorated the Fish-mas sea fan.

When there were no empty branches left, Shrimp swam up and placed the glowing starfish on the very top. "All done!" he exclaimed.

"The house is ready for Santa Paws," Mama purred.

"Good," Shrimp said. He yawned. "Because I'm ready for bed!"

"Good night, Shrimp," Coral said. "See you Fish-mas morning."

Shrimp blew some sleepy kisses and swam to his room. Coral took Shrimp's letter out of her backpack. Then she looked at Angel and Shelly. "It's almost time," she said. "We're going to get this letter to Santa Paws tonight. Then we can tell Shrimp all about the Fish-mas miracle!"

Shelly pointed at the clock on the wall. "But we have a few hours until Santa Paws will be here," Shelly said. "What should we do?"

"Can we watch a movie?" Angel asked. "*A Fish-mas Story* is my favorite."

"That's a great idea," Coral said. She carefully placed Shrimp's letter on the end table. Then she used the remote control to turn on the shell-ivision.

The first hour of the movie was great. But then Coral noticed that Shelly and Angel weren't laughing at the funny parts anymore. She turned to look at them. They were half asleep! "Angel! Shelly!" she shouted.

"What? Huh?" Shelly replied sleepily.

Angel just opened one eye and frowned.

"We're supposed to stay awake!" Coral said. She shook Angel's shoulder.

"We know, we know," Angel said. She sat up. Shelly did the same.

Mama poked her head into the room. "Are you girls getting tired?" she asked.

Angel rubbed her eyes. Shelly yawned. They both nodded. But Coral said, "No, we're fine."

"It's all right if you want to rest," Mama said.

Coral shook her head. "You know we're waiting for Santa Paws."

Mama nodded. "I'll check on you girls in a little bit," she purred.

Coral got off the sofa. She grabbed one of Angel's paws and one of Shelly's paws. "Let's play a game," she suggested.

"Do we have to?" Angel whined.

"It will help us stay awake," Coral replied. She pulled her friends up. "We can play hide-and-seek. I'll be it first."

Coral turned away from her friends and closed her eyes. She started counting to ten. But she was so tired she was afraid she'd fall asleep! *I'll just keep them covered,* she thought. She covered her face with her paws. Finally, she got to ten. "Ready or not, here I come!" she announced.

Coral turned around. Shelly and Angel weren't hiding! They had nodded off, this time in front of the Fish-mas sea fan.

Coral floated to her friends and gently shook them. "Wake up, you two," she said.

Shelly opened her eyes a little bit. Angel didn't move at all. "Just five more minutes, Coral," Shelly begged. Then she yawned and closed her eyes.

Coral sank down to the floor next to her sleeping friends. She felt exhausted. *But I have to stay awake!* She tapped her tail against the floor to keep from falling asleep. But the tapping got slower and slower.

Maybe I can rest my eyes for a minute, Coral thought. *Just one minute . . .*

9

"Meow-y Fish-mas, everyone!" Papa shouted.

Coral rubbed her eyes sleepily. "What did you say?" she asked.

"Meow-y Fish-mas!" Papa repeated. He swam over and pulled the blanket off his daughter.

Suddenly, Coral's eyes snapped open. "Wait! It's morning?"

Papa nodded. "You kittens were

sleeping so soundly, we couldn't even wake you to get Angel and Shelly home!" He chuckled. "It looks like they're still half asleep now."

"Your mothers are on their way over to pick you girls up," Mama said. "Your families miss you!"

They nodded sleepily. "We're getting up," Shelly mumbled.

Coral turned to the end table where she'd placed Shrimp's letter. It was still there. "Oh no!" she wailed.

Shelly and Angel heard their friend crying and immediately swam to her. "What happened?" Shelly asked.

Coral gulped. "It's Fish-mas morning. We didn't stay awake." She covered her face with her paws. "Santa Paws is already gone. We never gave him this letter."

Angel and Shelly gasped. "We didn't mean to fall asleep!" Angel cried.

Coral shrugged. "It doesn't matter what we meant to do," she mumbled.

Shelly put a paw around Coral's shoulders and squeezed. "It'll be all right," she purred.

"It's Fish-mas! It's Fish-mas! It's Fish-mas!" someone shouted. Coral spun around. It was Shrimp! He had a huge grin on his face. He looked very excited.

Coral felt terrible. *I have to tell him,* she thought. *I have to tell my brother that I ruined Fish-mas.*

Coral pulled away from Shelly. She swam over to Shrimp and squared her shoulders. She took a deep breath and said, "I'm so sorry."

"Sorry for what?" Shrimp asked. He saw his sister's tears. He reached up and wiped one away. Then he held Coral's paws. "Don't cry, Coral. It's Fish-mas! There's no reason to cry on Fish-mas."

"I missed Santa Paws," Coral sobbed. "I fell asleep, so I couldn't give him your letter, Shrimp."

Shrimp's mouth fell open. He let go of

Coral's paws. "B-b-but you purr-omised," he stammered.

"I know," Coral said. "I messed up."

"She tried her best to stay awake," Angel said.

"We all did," Shelly added.

Shrimp sniffled. "It's fine," he said. "It's not a big deal. I'll just write to Santa Paws next year."

He was being very understanding. Which made Coral feel even worse.

Mama swam to Shrimp and gave him a hug. "I know you're upset," she purred, "but let's go look under the sea fan. Santa Paws may surprise you."

"That sounds like a great idea," Papa said. "I think we should all go check the Fish-mas sea fan."

Mama led Shrimp away. But Coral slumped down to the floor. She stared sadly at Shrimp's letter.

"I know you feel bad," Angel said, "but maybe we should try to do something fun."

Coral sighed. "I just don't feel very Fish-mas-y right now."

"You know, Coral," Papa said, sitting down next to her, "what you did last night was the most Fish-mas-y thing I've seen in a while."

"What do you mean?" Coral asked. "All I did was fall asleep early and ruin everything."

"Actually," Papa said, "you tried to do something nice for someone you love. You did your best to spread Fish-mas spirit. That's what Fish-mas is really about."

Coral shook her head. "I didn't want Fish-mas spirit," she whined. "I wanted Fish-mas *magic*!"

Papa kissed Coral's forehead. "I think it was purr-ty magical. Maybe you'll see that someday, too."

Tears flowed down Coral's cheeks. *This was supposed to be the best Fish-mas,* she thought, *but it's turning out to be the worst.*

"Let's open some presents," Shelly suggested. "That will make you feel better. I'll find my gift for you."

"I'll get mine, too," Angel added. "We'll bring them here."

Coral shrugged.

Shelly reached for the letter on the table. "I'm just going to move this," she said. "We don't need it here to remind us—" She stopped in the middle of her sentence and gasped.

"What is it?" Angel asked. She rushed over. "You look like you've seen a sea spider!"

"Look at this!" Shelly exclaimed. She held up a red envelope. "This was under Shrimp's letter."

"It's for you, Coral," Angel said.

"I don't understand," Coral said. She

reached out, and Shelly handed her the envelope. She ripped it open and took out a letter. *"Dear Coral,"* she read.

I'm sorry that you were sleeping last night when I visited your house. I would have liked to meet you!

Trying to stay up to give me Shrimp's letter was a very nice thing to do. You must really love your brother!

The next time you write to me, please tell me if I got everything right for him.

Love,
Santa Paws

P.S. You're very lucky to have friends like Shelly and Angel. I wish I could have met them, too.

P.P.S. Did you know that Angel snores?

"I do not!" Angel exclaimed, scowling.

But Coral didn't hear her. She couldn't believe what she was reading!

"Santa Paws says to tell him if he got everything right for Shrimp," Shelly said. "But what does that mean?"

Coral scratched her head. "I don't know," she said. "His letter is still here. So Santa Paws couldn't have seen it."

Just then, the girls heard Shrimp yelling, "Coral! Come here! Look!"

10

Coral rushed toward Shrimp. Her friends followed close behind. They found him in front of the Fish-mas sea fan.

"Is everything all right?" Coral asked her brother.

"Look!" Shrimp answered. He was hovering in front of a new drum. "Santa Paws got me exactly what I asked for!" he said.

Coral scratched her head. She looked

at her parents. "Did you get the drum for Shrimp?" she asked.

"Are you squidding?" Papa purred. "Parents don't buy drums for kittens. Think of the noise!"

"It was Santa Paws!" Shrimp cried. He waved a red envelope like the one Coral had just opened. "I got this, too. It's a letter from Santa Paws. It says, *Your sister worked very hard to make sure I would know how to make your Fish-mas wishes come true. Purrmaids like her spread Fish-mas spirit as well as I can. Make sure you thank her! Love, Santa Paws.*" He wrapped his arms around Coral's waist and squeezed. "I can't believe it! You *did* get my letter to Santa Paws!"

"I can't believe it, either," Coral replied. "I don't know how it happened."

"It must have been Fish-mas magic," Angel suggested.

"That's the only explanation!" Shelly added.

Shrimp squeezed Coral again. "You really are the best sister!" he said.

"Well, I *do* believe that!" Coral said, giggling. "Especially since I'm *still* your only sister."

All the purrmaids laughed. Shrimp, Coral, Shelly, and Angel began to give out the presents that were left under the Fish-mas sea fan. "Santa Paws brought so many gifts!" Shelly said.

Coral spied something poking out from under the lowest branch. She leaned down and picked it up. It was a small box wrapped in gold seaweed.

"What is that?" Shelly asked.

"And who is it for?" Angel added.

Coral looked for the tag. It read, *To Coral and her paw-some friends, Shelly and Angel. Love, Santa Paws.* "It's for the three of us. From Santa Paws!"

"Open it!" Shelly squealed.

Coral ripped the seaweed off as quickly as Angel would have. She opened the lid of the box. Inside, there were three tiny cone shells. Each one was painted red and had tiny pearls around the bottom edge. There was a tiny pearl on top of each. "These look just like the ornament I made for Ms. Harbor!" Coral gasped.

"But they're not ornaments," Angel said. She lifted one shell up. "Look! There's a little clip on each one."

"Which means we can put these on our friendship bracelets!" Shelly exclaimed.

"That's a fin-tastic idea," Coral agreed. "That way we'll always remember the most important thing."

"That presents are paw-some?" Angel joked.

Coral grinned and shook her head. "No," she purred. "These charms will remind us that Fish-mas wishes do come true!"

The purrmaids are going on their first sleepover field trip!

Turn the page for a sneak peek!

By the time the lunch bell rang, the students of Eel-Twelve couldn't stop talking about the meteor shower.

Angel always found it hard to float still. There were just too many things to do! Today, she ate her lunch more quickly than Shelly or Coral had ever seen.

"Slow down, Angel," Coral warned. "You're going to make yourself sick!"

"I can't slow down!" Angel exclaimed. "I'm too excited! This is going to be the best field trip!"

Shelly nodded. "I think you're right," she said.

"Did you two bring everything on the packing list?" Coral asked. She pointed to a backpack that matched her soft orange fur. "I've double-checked my bag. But maybe I should check yours, too. I don't want us to forget anything important."

"Coral is always so worried about following the rules," Shelly whispered into Angel's ear. Coral usually tried to keep the girls out of trouble. It was one of the things Angel loved about her friend.

"Here's my bag," Angel purred. "I definitely packed my new octopus pajamas. But maybe you can check for everything else."

Coral started looking through it right away. Angel held her paw in front of her mouth so Coral wouldn't see her smile.

Shelly placed her bag on the floor next to Coral. "Here's mine," she said. Then she grinned. "I can't believe we get to go camping. Overnight!"

"*I* can't believe we'll be hanging out at the surface of the water!" Angel exclaimed.

Purrmaids didn't go to the surface often. It wasn't always safe there. They spent most of their lives deep under the sea. In fact, there were lots of purrmaids in Kittentail Cove who'd never been to the surface!

Angel was lucky. She and her best friends had been to the surface a few times. The first time was when the girls visited Siren Island and saw narwhals. Another time was when Ms. Harbor took the class to Coastline Farm.

But today was even more special. The class wasn't just going to visit the surface. They were going to stay there for hours! Angel couldn't wait.